Gittel's Hands

by Erica Silverman • pictures by Deborah Nourse Lattimore

BridgeWater Paperback

Published by BridgeWater Paperback,
an imprint and trademark of Troll Communications L.L.C.

Designed by Aileen Friedman.

First published in hardcover by BridgeWater Books.

First paperback edition published 1998.

Printed in the United States of America.

10 9 8 7 6 5 4 3 2 1

Library of Congress Cataloging-in-Publication Data

Silverman, Erica.
Gittel's hands / Erica Silverman: pictures by Deborah Nourse Lattimore.
p.   cm.
Summary: Yakov boasts of his daughter's abilities but doesn't
allow Gittel to speak for herself until the day she makes an Elijah
cup that amazes even her father.
ISBN 0-8167-3798-3 (lib. bdg.)   ISBN 0-8167-3799-1 (pbk.)
1. Jews—Europe—Juvenile fiction.
[1. Elijah (Biblical prophet)—Fiction.
2. Jews—Europe—Fiction.
3. Fathers and daughters—Fiction.]
I. Lattimore, Deborah Nourse, ill.   II. Title.
PZ7.S58625Gi 1996 [E]—dc20   96-3625

To my father, Harold, and my grandfather, Jacob, in loving memory. — E.S.

To Erica, whose lovely hands and heart gave me this story to illustrate;
and to Bonnie and Aileen, with thanks and affection. — D.N.L.

$\mathcal{L}$ong ago, there was a man known as Yakov the water carrier. He lived with his daughter, Gittel, in a little house in a shtetl at the foot of the Carpathian Mountains. Yakov loved to talk, and Gittel, being a good daughter, knew how to listen.

She listened as she cooked and baked, embroidered and sewed. Gittel was always working with her hands. From rags and scraps, she made toys for the orphans and scarves for the beggars.

Everything Gittel did was a wonder in her father's eyes. Yakov the water carrier boasted and bragged about her to everyone he met.

"My daughter made me a prayer shawl good enough for Elijah the prophet!" Yakov told the shoemaker.

Gittel blushed. "It's a plain prayer shawl, Papa," she said quietly.

"Her noodle pudding is like manna from heaven!" he told the feather plucker.

Gittel lowered her eyes. "Just an ordinary noodle pudding."

He greeted the rabbi's wife. "Have you seen the work of my Gittel's hands?"

"Papa, please," whispered Gittel.

Yakov raised his voice. "Her candlesticks are like nothing you've ever seen!"

"Such talk!" The rabbi's wife wrinkled her brow. "Be careful with your words, Reb Yakov. Don't you know that boasting brings bad luck?"

"Who's boasting?" replied Yakov. "Every word is true."

The rabbi's wife wagged a finger in warning. "Words once spoken are like little dybbuks. They dance around. They cause all kinds of trouble."

Yakov laughed. "Such foolishness! I am not afraid of words."

That year, winter lingered. Snow clung to the ground even as Gittel began to prepare for the spring holiday of Passover. Shivering beneath her shawl, she washed the walls. She scrubbed the special plates and pots and utensils used only during Passover. She prepared dough for matzo and brought it to the baker's oven.

One day she was embroidering a matzo cover when her father came home for his midday meal.

"The winter's hay is gone," he said sadly. "And the hay merchant demands that I pay him the forty rubles I still owe."

"Couldn't we pay him in some other way? The apple vendor once paid you with apples." Her eyes searched the sparsely furnished room.

Yakov hung his head. "What do I have that Reb Raya would want? Water? He has his own well!" Suddenly his eyes lit up. "Child, come with me."

Yakov harnessed his horse to the wagon and took Gittel to the grand home of Reb Raya, the hay merchant. "Be silent," he commanded. "Let me do the talking."

Reb Raya opened the door.

"Good day, Reb Raya," said Yakov. "When you see the magnificent work of my daughter's hands, you will be pleased to have her sew for you. In this way will we pay for our hay."

"I employ the services of a superior seamstress," Reb Raya replied.

"But Gittel is even better," insisted Yakov. "From nothing more than an old rag and a piece of thread, she can embroider a perfect matzo cover."

"Oh, Papa, no!" thought Gittel. She tugged at his sleeve.

But words once spoken are like little dybbuks. They dance around. They cause all kinds of trouble.

"Better?" said the hay merchant. "If what you say is true, your daughter can certainly work for me. If not, I will take your water barrel. That will pay for some of my hay."

Reb Raya led Gittel to the parlor. He gave her a piece of cloth and a spool of thread. "I will return in one hour."

"Please, may I have a needle for sewing?" asked Gittel.

"Your father said nothing of needles," he replied. And he locked the door.

Gittel searched the parlor, but she could not find a sewing needle anywhere.

The sound of wings flapping frantically inside the chimney startled her. Looking up the flue, she saw a trapped dove. She reached in and very gently pulled it out. Trembling, the dove nipped at its oily feathers.

"Little dove," said Gittel, "I cannot make a matzo cover without a needle, but at least I can help you." And she wiped its feathers clean of soot and ash.

Then she held open a narrow window. As she watched the dove fly off, she thought she saw something moving in the courtyard. "Who is out there?" she wondered.

Suddenly the parlor door opened. In strode Reb Raya, followed by Yakov.

"Aha! Just as I thought," said Reb Raya. "There is no matzo cover! The barrel is now mine."

"How can this be?" Yakov cried.

"Papa, let me explain!" pleaded Gittel.

"Sha! Be silent!" said Yakov. "I will take care of this." He turned to Reb Raya. "Never mind the sewing. My daughter can cook!"

Reb Raya rolled his eyes. "I have the best cook in town."

"Gittel is better," insisted Yakov. "From a few table scraps, she can prepare a holiday feast!"

Gittel tapped her father's shoulder. "Papa . . . ," she whispered.

But words once spoken are like little dybbuks. They dance around. They cause all kinds of trouble.

"If she cannot do as you say, I will take your wagon. That will pay for some of my hay."

In the kitchen, Reb Raya gave Gittel one egg, a half cup of milk, and a small chunk of cheese. He locked the pantry. "I will return in one hour."

"Please, may I have firewood for cooking?" asked Gittel.

"Your father said nothing of wood." And he locked the door.

Searching for firewood, Gittel heard a whimpering noise. A cat, thin as a stick, climbed onto the window ledge.

"Little cat, I cannot cook without firewood," she said. "But at least I can feed you."

She set the cheese, the milk, and the egg before the cat and watched it eat. From somewhere outside, Gittel heard footsteps. Her eyes searched the courtyard. "Someone is out there," she said to the cat. The cat blinked its green eyes at her.

Just then the door opened. In strode Reb Raya, followed by Yakov.

"Just as I thought!" said the hay merchant. "The wagon is mine!"

Yakov ran after him. "Please, give us one more chance."

"Papa, I must explain," said Gittel.

"It is time for you to be silent."

Yakov turned to Reb Raya. "Perhaps the cooking did not go well. But my Gittel makes cups and plates and candlesticks. In fact, she could even make a silver Elijah's cup if she had some silver!"

"Papa, please," murmured Gittel. But words once spoken are like little dybbuks. They dance around. They cause all kinds of trouble.

"Fine," said Reb Raya quickly. "If she can do as you say, she may work for me. If not, your horse will be mine. And my hay will be paid for."

Reb Raya led Gittel to the cellar and handed her a silver coin. "You have until the sun sets."

Gittel paced back and forth. "Without his wagon, his barrel, and his horse, my father will have nothing. If only I could help him. . . ." She stared out the window.

Suddenly from out of the shadows of the courtyard stepped an old beggar, shivering with cold.

"I can't seem to help my father," said Gittel, "but at least this might give you warmth." And she offered him her shawl.

The beggar took it. Then with a wave of his hand . . .

. . . he was standing before her in the cellar. The green-eyed cat circled his feet. On his shoulder perched the dove. Suddenly a workbench appeared —and tools—and bars of pure silver. Flames flickered in the hearth.

Outside, the sun stopped in its path.
The beggar showed Gittel how to make candlesticks and seder plates.
And he watched in silent approval as she made a graceful Elijah's cup.

The beggar looked deeply into Gittel's eyes.

Never had she seen such compassion. And she knew then that she stood before Elijah the prophet. She trembled. "How can I ever thank you?" she whispered.

Elijah smiled. "With the work of your hands, with the goodness of your heart, and with the wisdom of your words." Then he disappeared.

Where he had stood, the air still shimmered. In the hearth lay one silver coin.

Outside, the sun sank behind the hills.

The cellar door opened. In strode Reb Raya, followed by Yakov.

Reb Raya's eyes opened wide.

Yakov, too, gazed in wonder at his daughter and the beautiful things she had made.

"I told you she's capable. Why my daughter can—"

"Your daughter can work for me," said Reb Raya. "Starting today! She will make silver goods, and I will sell them." He held out his hand.

The water carrier reached to shake it. "My daughter will be happy to work for you!"

"Papa, stop!" cried Gittel. And she stepped between them. "I have listened well. Now, with your permission, I will speak."

The water carrier stared at his daughter.

"Because I had neither needle for sewing nor firewood for cooking," said Gittel, "this man cheated you out of your barrel and your wagon. I could never work for him." She gathered up all that she'd made and headed outside. Yakov followed.

"Wait, please!" The hay merchant ran after them. "You can have your barrel and your wagon. And here is some hay for your horse."

"My dear Reb Yakov," he added, "you are the girl's father. Tell her
she must work for me."

Yakov smiled proudly. "My daughter speaks for herself," he replied.
"And she does it better than anyone else."

From that time forth, people came from miles around to admire the work of Gittel's hands. They bought her finely wrought candlesticks, her intricate seder plates, and especially her graceful Elijah's cups.

It was whispered that Elijah himself had been her teacher.

But don't you repeat it. For words once spoken are like little dybbuks. They dance around. They cause all kinds of trouble.

Here are some words from the story...

Passover A spring holiday celebrated to remember the time long ago when the Jewish people escaped from slavery in Egypt.

Shtetl A small, Eastern European village.

Dybbuk A mischievous demon.

Matzo A flat bread or cracker eaten during Passover to symbolize the escape of the Jewish slaves, who did not have time for their bread to rise.

Matzo cover A decorated cloth that covers the matzo.

Elijah In Jewish folktales, the prophet Elijah is a loving and magical spirit who helps poor, kind-hearted people in time of trouble.

Elijah's cup A distinctive goblet, often made of silver, filled with wine for Elijah the prophet. At a specific moment in the Passover seder, the door of the home is opened and Elijah is invited in.

Seder A sacred dinner and ceremony during which the story of Passover is told with readings, songs, and prayers.

Seder plate An ornately decorated plate, holding some of the Passover foods that remind people of the sadness of slavery and the joy of freedom.